P9-BBP-789

"HELLO READING books are a perfect introduction to reading. Brief sentences full of word repetition and full-color pictures stress visual clues to help a child take the first important steps toward reading. Mastering these story books will build children's reading confidence and give them the enthusiasm to stand on their own in the world of words."

—Bee Cullinan
Past President of the International Reading
Association, Professor in New York University's
Early Childhood and Elementary Education Program

"Readers aren't born, they're made. Desire is planted—planted by parents who work at it."

—Jim Trelease
author of *The Read Aloud Handbook*

"When I was a classroom reading teacher, I recognized the importance of good stories in making children understand that reading is more than just recognizing words. I saw that children who have ready access to story books get excited about reading. They also make noticeably greater gains in reading comprehension. The development of the HELLO READING stories grows out of this experience."

—Harriet Ziefert
M.A.T., New York University School of Education
Author, Language Arts Module,
Scholastic Early Childhood Program

For Ing Hoffman and Anna Burton,
good mothers, good physicians

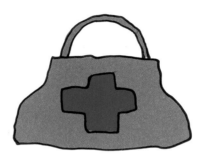

PUFFIN BOOKS
Published by the Penguin Group
Viking Penguin Inc., 40 West 23rd Street, New York, New York 10010, U.S.A.
Penguin Books Ltd, 27 Wrights Lane, London W8 5TZ, England
Penguin Books Australia Ltd, Ringwood, Victoria, Australia
Penguin Books Canada Ltd, 2801 John Street, Markham, Ontario, Canada L3R 1B4
Penguin Books (N.Z.) Ltd, 182-190 Wairau Road, Auckland 10, New Zealand

Penguin Books Ltd, Registered Offices: Harmondsworth, Middlesex, England

First published in Puffin Books, 1989 • Published simultaneously in Canada

1 3 5 7 9 10 8 6 4 2

Text copyright © Harriet Ziefert, 1989
Illustrations copyright © Suzy Mandel, 1989
All rights reserved
Library of Congress catalog card number: 88-62152
ISBN 0-14-050985-2

Printed in Singapore for Harriet Ziefert, Inc.

Except in the United States of America, this book is sold subject to the condition that it
shall not, by way of trade or otherwise, be lent, re-sold, hired out, or otherwise
circulated without the publisher's prior consent in any form of binding or cover other
than that in which it is published and without a similar condition including this
condition being imposed on the subsequent purchaser.

DR. CAT

Harriet Ziefert
Pictures by Suzy Mandel

PUFFIN BOOKS

Ring! Ring!
Ring-a-ling!

Wake up, Dr. Cat!

Dr. Cat went
into the bathroom.

He combed his whiskers.

Then he got dressed.

He put on pants...

a shirt...

a tie...

and a white coat.

Dr. Cat put his bag
on his bike.

He rode to his office.

"Good morning, Dr. Cat,"
said Tim, Jim, and Kim.

"Good morning, Dr. Cat,"
said the nurse.

"Who's first today?"
asked Dr. Cat.

"Not me!" said Tim.
"Not me!" said Jim.
"Not me!" said Kim.

"Somebody has to be first,"
said Dr. Cat.

"Tim and Jim will be first,"
said their mother.

"You first!" said Tim to Jim.
"You first!" said Jim to Tim.

"I'll be first," said Dr. Cat.

So Tim checked Dr. Cat's right ear.
And Jim checked his left ear.

Then Dr. Cat checked
Tim and Jim.

He checked their ears.
He checked their noses.

"Now I'm going to check throats," said Dr. Cat. "Who's first?"

"You first!" said Tim to Jim.
"You first!" said Jim to Tim.

"I'll be first!" said Dr. Cat.
So Tim and Jim checked Dr. Cat.
"AHH!" said Dr. Cat. "AHH!"

And Dr. Cat checked Tim and Jim.
"Ahhh!" said Tim.

"Ahhhhhh!" said Jim.

"Let me listen first," cried Tim.
"No, me first!" said Jim.

"I'm first," said Dr. Cat.

Dr. Cat listened
to Tim's heart beat.
Ker-thump! Ker-thump!

Then he listened
to Jim's heart beat.
Ker-thump! Ker-thump!

"Give Jim a shot!" said Tim.

"No shots today!" said Dr. Cat.
"But who wants to peek inside
my doctor bag?"

"Me first!" said Tim.
"No, me first!" said Jim.

"They can look together,"
said their mother.

"Good idea!" said Dr. Cat.
"Then you're both first!"